Uraoooligan Lukwherurdriven!Gerraftberode!

Eeeaswoscrreech!!!!

Spprrutt
Pftpt
Brrrpptt

Schluuupglubshuprrglub

QWARYOUALRITEDEN

Pftpt Frrrupptt

Pisshpusshawertt

Eyenolessgofurawark

D1397045

GRANDPA'S NOISES

First published 2019

EK Books
an imprint of Exisle Publishing Pty Ltd
PO Box 864, Chatswood, NSW 2057, Australia
226 High Street, Dunedin, 9016, New Zealand
www.ekbooks.org

Copyright © 2019 in text: Gareth St John Thomas
Copyright © 2019 in illustrations: Colin Rowe

Gareth St John Thomas and Colin Rowe assert the moral right to be identified
as the creators of this work.

All rights reserved. Except for short extracts for the purpose of review, no part of
this book may be reproduced, stored in a retrieval system or transmitted in any
form or by any means, whether electronic, mechanical, photocopying, recording
or otherwise, without prior written permission from the publisher.

A CiP record for this book is available from the National Library of Australia.

ISBN 978-1-925335-98-9

Designed by Big Cat Design
Typeset in Warnock Pro 18/25pt
Printed in China

This book uses paper sourced under ISO 14001 guidelines from well-managed
forests and other controlled sources.

10 9 8 7 6 5 4 3 2 1

For Nathan.
— G.S.J.T.

For my Mum and Dad.
— C.R.

GRANDPA'S NOISES

Gareth St John Thomas & Colin Rowe

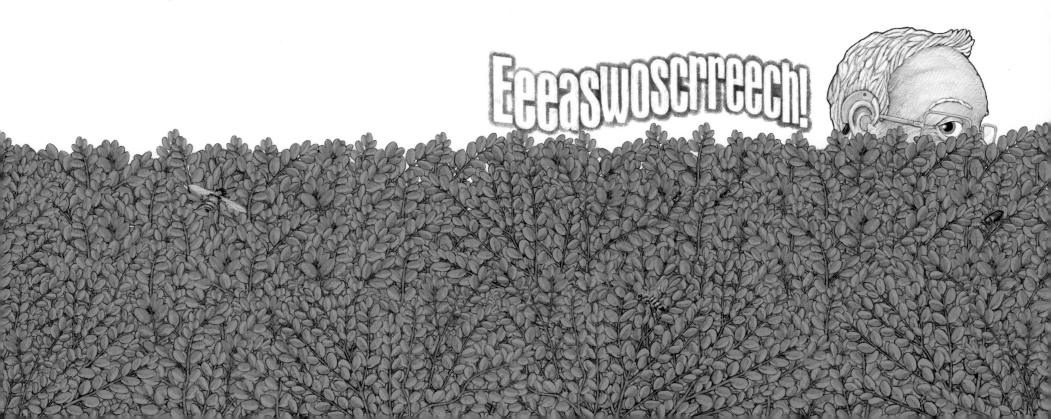

Eeeaswoscrreech!

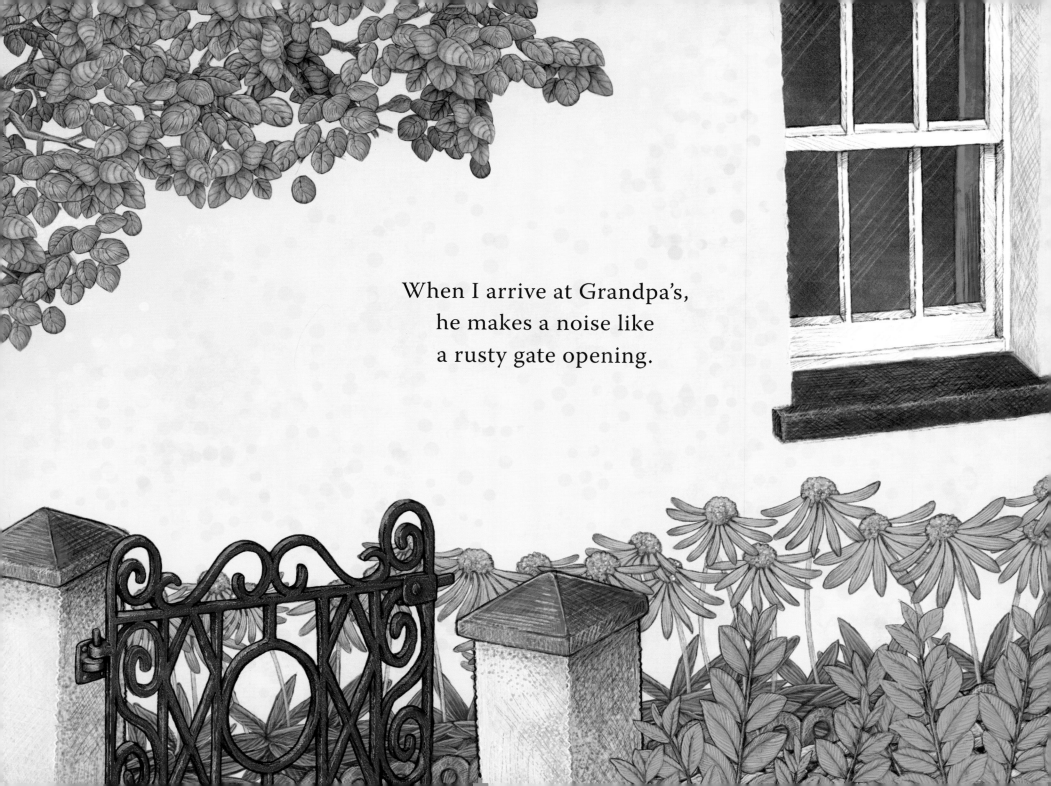

When I arrive at Grandpa's,
he makes a noise like
a rusty gate opening.

Eeeeaarrrlllooo

That means hello.

When he sits down,
his knees grumble
about having to work.

Crack crack

As he drinks his cup of tea,
he makes a noise like
a busy drain.

And when he's finished,
Grandpa sounds like a
balloon that's leaking air.

Aaahhh

That means he
liked his tea.

If it's not raining, he'll often make a long rumbling sound.

Eyenolessgofurawark

That means he thinks we should go for a walk.

As he stands up, his knees complain and his back joins in.

After he's put on his coat and found
his stick and we've closed the door ...

... he stops for a moment.

Pisshpusshawertt

That means he's found
getting ready a little tiring.

Frurruppptt Brrrppftt Spprrutt Pft

As we walk, his bottom makes a lot of noises.

Dad's makes those noises too.

Sometimes, when a noisy car goes past us, a noise comes out of his ear.

That's his hearing aid.

When he meets one
of his friends, we stop
so they can chat.

Owaryoualriteden
Nobadataltanksfurasken

They always ask
how each other is,
and they always
seem to be fine.

Once when we were out walking, a car drove through a puddle and splashed us.

Grandpa made lots of noises then.

Uraoooligan!
Lukwherurdriven!
Gerrofftherode!

RAARRGGGGGHH!

He waved his stick at the car
and went a bit red in the face.
He roared like a lion.

His bottom got excited too.

Frrrupppttt Brrrppff
Spprrutt Pftpt

It was so loud that his hearing aid joined in. Grandpa wasn't happy at all that his coat was wet.

His bottom wouldn't stop complaining either.

Frrruppptt Brrrppfft Spprrutt Pffpt
Spprrutt Pffpt Brrrppfft
Pffpt Frrruppptt Spprrutt Brrrppfft
Brrrppfft Spprrutt Pffpt Frrruppptt

Back home, Grandpa sat
down in his chair.

He put his finger in his ear
and waggled it around.

Then he picked up a tissue ...

just in time!

Aaaaaaatchoooooooooooo!

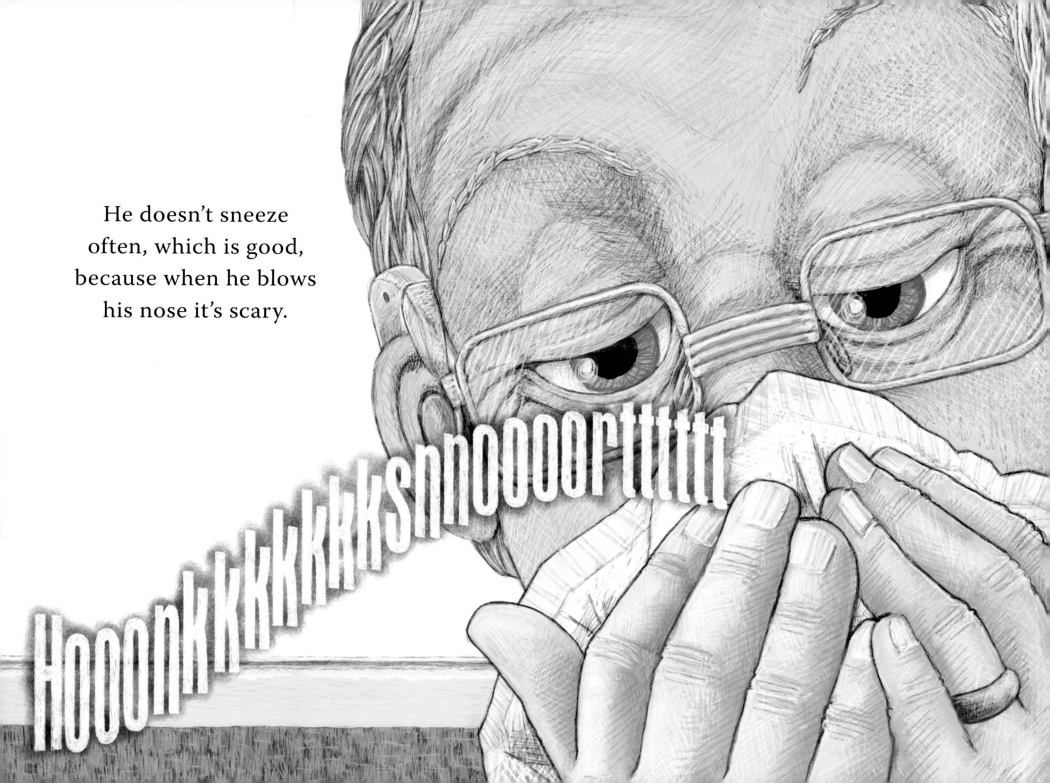

He doesn't sneeze often, which is good, because when he blows his nose it's scary.

Hooonkkkkkkkhksnnoooorttttt

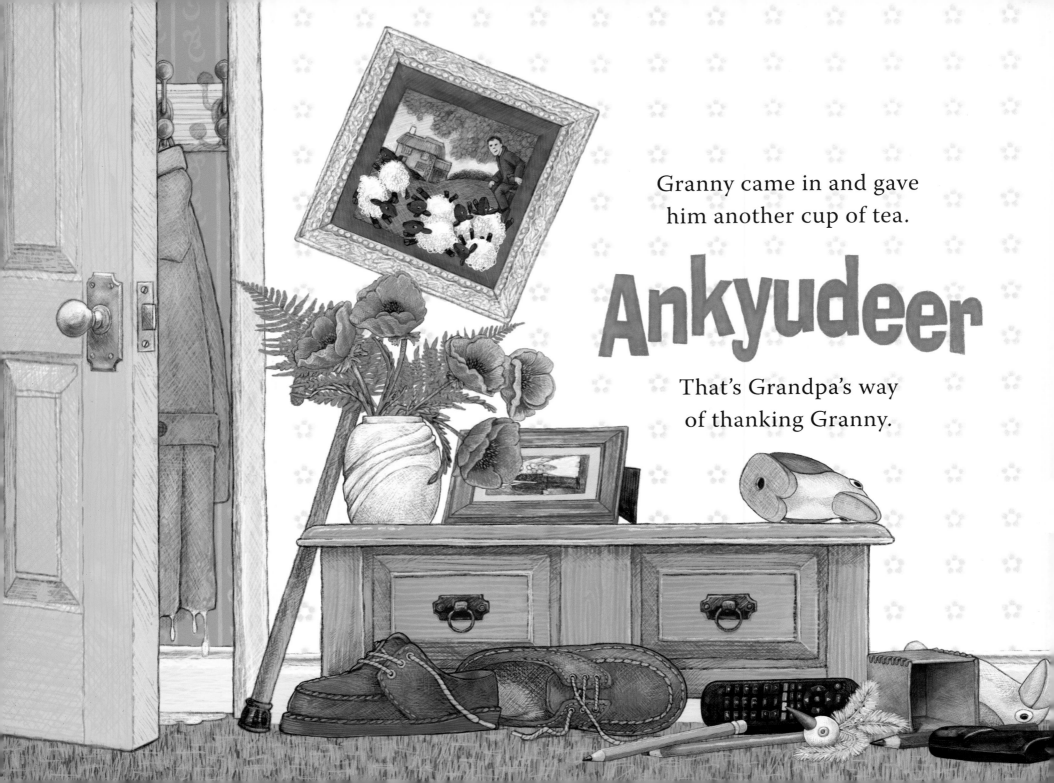

Granny came in and gave
him another cup of tea.

Ankyudeer

That's Grandpa's way
of thanking Granny.

The tea was a good idea of
Granny's. Soon Grandpa was
settled in his chair again,
happy and relaxed.

Purrrr

Grandpa makes a lot of noises but I understand
most of them so we get on just fine.

aaaaaaatchoooooooo! Ankyudeer Creak
Pop
RAARRGgGGHH! purrrrrrr
Frrrupppttt Eeeaarrrlloo Aaahh
Brrrppfft
Spprrutt CRACK
Pfft... CRACK
HOOonkkkkkkksnnooorttttt